SHOUT OUT LOUD!
2
高口里純

C O N T E N T S

Shout Out Loud #4 ----------- 3
Shout Out Loud #5 --------- 63
Shout Out Loud #6 ---------121
Post script--------------------173

In order to maintain as much authenticity as possible,
Shout Out Loud retains the original Japanese name order for all names.
Thus family name comes first, followed by the given name.
The series will also retain honorifics.

IN THE NEW ANIME SHOW ON TOUZAI TELEVISION, MIRACLE DIETER MIYUKI...
...I, HISAE SHINO, NABBED A MAJOR SUPPORTING ROLE.
THE MAIN CHARACTER IS A SLIGHTLY CHUBBY MAGICAL GIRL.
MY SON NAKAYA IS A HEALTHY 17 YEAR-OLD HIGH SCHOOLER.
SHOUT OUT LOUD!

MIYUKI-CHAN IS SO CUTE...

ER...AT LEAST HE'S SUPPOSED TO BE.
HUH?!
SHOUT OUT LOUD!™

Miracle Dieter MIYUKI
WHY THE LONG FACE, HISAE-SAN?
HUH?
OH... MIZUSAWA-KUN...
SOMETHING GOT YOU DOWN?
NO, IT'S NOTHING...

SOMETHING ABOUT YOUR SON, PERHAPS?
UH...
AH...
THERE'S WORD GOING AROUND THAT MIZUSAWA SWINGS THE OTHER WAY.
YOU TWO'VE BEEN PAIRED UP A LOT RECENTLY, HAVEN'T YOU?
A-HA!
I GOT IT.
YOU MUST HAVE TENRYU-SAN ON YOUR MIND THEN, EH?
WHAT?!
SHAME ON YOU, HISAE-SAN!
WE'RE RECORDING A CHILDREN'S SHOW HERE. NO X-RATED THOUGHTS, PLEASE.

EXCUSE ME?!
WHO EVER SAID ANYTHING ABOUT X-RATED THOUGHTS, MIZUSAWA-KUN?!
SHINO-SAN. YOUR TONE IS GIVING YOU AWAY.
GOOD MORNING!
HEH HEH.
YOU REALLY ARE ADORABLE, HISAE-SAN.
~
YOU TWO SURE ARE CLOSE. SHINO-SAN.
LISTEN HERE, AYA-CHAN!
YES, MY DEAR?
GOOD MORNING!
Y'know, I've been meaning to tell you. I've been looking forward to my chance to work opposite you, Shino-san.
HANAMAKI-SAN!
UM...!

OH... GOOD MORNING.
HANAMAKI CHIZURU. AGE 28. SIX YEARS OF VOICE ACTING EXPERIENCE.
UH...I WAS JUST WONDERING IF YOU WOULD GIVE ME YOUR AUTOGRAPH?
OH, OF COURSE!
SO IS THIS FOR YOUR NIECE OR SOME-THING?
SHOULD I ADD HER NAME?
NO... UH... CAN YOU WRITE IT OUT TO NA-KAYA-KUN?
OH MY!
YOUR NEPHEW?
To Nakaya-kun
はは
HERE YOU GO!

AH...
THANKS SO MUCH...
I CAN'T TELL HER IT'S ACTUALLY MY SON...
"LET'S DO IT!"
"DUMBBELL ACTION..."
"...GO!!"

YOU LISTENING, NAKAYA?
HUH?
`SUP, KUNI-WAKI?
......
I'LL JUST GO BY MYSELF, THEN.
カタン
WAIT! WHERE'RE YOU GOING?!
TODAY'S THE PRACTICE GAME AGAINST JOUSEI HIGH.
OH...
DIDN'T YOU...
...PROMISE COACH SUGARAI YOU'D GO?
OH THAT'S RIGHT... TOTALLY FORGOT.
HEH HEH...
NAKA--

To Nakaya-kun
はなまき
ちずる
IT'S HANAMAKI CHIZURU'S AUTOGRAPH! ♡
AND THAT'S... WHO?
YOU DON'T KNOW?! SHE'S MIYUKI-CHAN FROM MIRACLE DIETER MIYUKI!!
SHINO GOT IT FOR ME.
MIYUKI-CHAN IS SERIOUSLY THE CUTEST THING EVER!
I'll never hand it over, Kuniwaki.
...I'M DEFINITELY GOING BY MYSELF.
SIGH...
TAKE IT EASY WITH THE LIQUOR THERE, SHINO.

TENRYU-SAN...
YOU CAME ALONE? HOW UNUSUAL.
SO, YOUR SON DOING WELL?
HA HA HA...
SURE.
......
ABOUT NAKAYA ...
HM?
YOU KNOW THAT HE PLAYS ICE HOCKEY, RIGHT?
YEAH ...
YOU SAID HE'S PRETTY GOOD.
THAT WAS BECAUSE HE WAS SO FOCUSED.

WHAT AM I GONNA DO, TENRYU-SAN?!
~
...WAS?
HEY! WATCH IT! WHAT'S THE MATTER WITH YOU?!
GRR!
NO NEED TO GET JEALOUS, BOY.
Huh? Wha?
OOOH, LOOKIE HERE!
SO MUCH FOR YOUR LITTLE PRIVATE MOMENT.

HE'S OBSESSED WITH MIRACLE DIETER MIYUKI?
HUH. NOW I GET IT.
SO THAT'S WHY YOU GOT HANAMAKI'S AUTOGRAPH EARLIER.
SO WHAT'S WRONG WITH THAT?
IT'S LIKE YOU AND YOUR SON GET TO HAVE SOMETHING IN COMMON.
WHO WOULD WANT TO HAVE THIS IN COMMON?!
WHY NOT, THOUGH?
NAKAYA'S SUPPOSED TO BE A NORMAL HIGH SCHOOL BOY. GETTING THIS ABSORBED IN SOME TWO-DIMENSIONAL GIRL, LET ALONE SOME ANIME CHARACTER...IT'S JUST NOT RIGHT!
AND IT'S A KIDDY-ANIME NO LESS!
OF THE MAGICAL GIRL VARIETY...
YOU'RE THE ONE WORKING ON IT, OLD MAN.
This is your kiddy-anime, remember?

AT LEAST THIS'S PROBABLY HEALTHIER THAN GETTING INTO THE YAOI CDS YOU'VE WORKED ON.
ギクッ
HANAMAKI'S CERTAINLY QUITE THE CHARACTER, THOUGH.
SHE'S 28 YEARS OLD AND STILL PUTTING HER HAIR UP IN PIGTAILS WITH POMPOMS?
And she's got the voice of a grade-schooler.
IF YOU SAY THAT, TENRYU-SAN...
...DON'T FORGET OUR HISAE-SAN HERE...
...WHO LOOKS AND SOUNDS ABOUT THE SAME AGE AS HIS HIGH-SCHOOLER SON!
THAT'S PLENTY ECCENTRIC, DON'T YOU THINK?
High schooler?
POINT TAKEN.

Y-YOU SHOULD KNOW THIS!
SORRY.
I AM NOT A HIGH SCHOOLER, MIZUSAWA-KUN!
Except for my voice...
BUT JUST YESTERDAY WE MADE SUCH SWEET SCHOOLMATES ...
How cold!
OH WELL ...
I WOULDN'T WORRY ABOUT IT TOO MUCH. IT'S JUST A PHASE.
I'm suddenly so tired.
JUST WHAT DID YOU COME HERE FOR THEN?
MI--!
WELL, I GOTTA GET UP EARLY TOMOR-ROW.

I SUPPOSE SO...
BESIDES ...
I USED TO BE SO WORRIED ABOUT NAKAYA BEING IN DANGER ON THAT ICE RINK.
HE'S ALREADY LOST A TOOTH...
...AND GETS INJURIES REGULARLY...
I HAD BEEN HOPING THAT HE'D TURN HIS ATTENTIONS...
...TOWARD SOMETHING A LITTLE LESS DANGEROUS.

EVERY TIME HE WOULD COME HOME WITH A FRESH INJURY, IT HURT ME JUST AS MUCH AS HIM.
?
Ow ow ow! The forehead and the cheek?!
WHAT CAN I SAY? I'M A PARENT.
BUT STILL...
GOOD MORNING.
OH... KUNIWAKI-KUN.
MORNING
OH, HEY POPS.
SALUTE
IS NAKAYA HERE?
OH, NAKAYA?
SORRY, BUT HE ALREADY LEFT.
WHAT?
CAN I HELP YOU?

THAT WEIRDO...
HE HASN'T BEEN PUTTING ANY ENERGY INTO HOCKEY AT ALL LATELY.
I THINK IT'S BECAUSE OF WHATEVER THAT ANIME IS THAT HE'S INTO...
ギク
I KNOW HE HAD HIS HEART SET ON COMING TO TERMS WITH HIS DAD'S JOB.
AND I THINK THAT'S FINE AND ALL...
BUT LOOKS LIKE IT'S GOTTEN A LITTLE OUTTA HAND.
Or something like that...
AND THIS IS SUCH AN IMPORTANT TIME FOR HIM--IT COULD DETERMINE WHETHER OR NOT HE GETS INTO JOUSEI HIGH.
し～ん
WHAAAAAAAT?!
PLUS, AT THIS RATE, HE'S GOING TO GET SERIOUSLY HURT.

WELL, THAT'S IT FROM ME!
Ku... Kuniwaki-kun?
......
WHAT SHOULD I DO?!
HE SAID HE'D BE COMING TO WATCH AT THE STUDIO AGAIN TODAY!!
SHINO!
A LITTLE LATE, AREN'T YOU?
YEAH...UH, I REALIZED I'D FORGOTTEN MY SCRIPT RIGHT WHEN I WAS ABOUT TO LEAVE.
AGAIN?
YOU CAN'T KEEP DOING THAT.
YOU'RE SUPPOSED TO BE A PROFES-SIONAL, REMEMBER?

GOOD MORNING.
MORNING, MIZUSAWA-KUN.
GOOD MORNING.
Dang... it's that annoying son of his...
`SCUSE ME!
Huh?
......

HEY, SHINO?
WHICH ONE'S HANAMAKI-SAN?
にま
OH... THERE SHE IS.
UH... LISTEN, NAKAYA.
OOOH!
HUH? WHAT'S UP?
......
IT'S JUST A PHASE.
"ISAMU-KUN."
"IF... IF I GOT THINNER, THEN..."
"WHAT'RE YOU TALKING ABOUT? YOU'RE PLENTY CUTE JUST THE WAY YOU ARE!"

"REALLY?"
"MIYUKI WILL NOT GIVE UP!"
YOU REALLY HAVE A COOL JOB, YOU KNOW THAT SHINO?
HUH?

I DIDN'T REALIZE IT UNTIL NOW...
...BUT VOICE ACTING IS LIKE ONE OF THOSE DREAM JOBS.
NAKAYA.
I'M GLAD YOU'RE A VOICE ACTOR, SHINO.
NOW I GET TO LISTEN TO MY FAVORITE CHARACTERS' VOICES UP CLOSE.
LIVING WITH MY SON AFTER 16 YEARS APART...
...HAS ITS ROUGH SPOTS, BUT I THINK WE'RE GETTING ALONG WELL.

I'M HAPPY HE'S INTERESTED IN WHAT I DO.
IF...
I'M HAPPY, BUT IT'S COMPLI-CATED...
IF NAKAYA REALLY GOT SERIOUSLY INJURED DURING HOCKEY...
Let's grab a bite before we go home.
...WOULDN'T IT BE MY FAULT?

NAKAYA!
YOU'RE TOO SOFT ON YOUR CHECK!
I KNOW, DAMMIT!
SHHU!

WHOA...!
ALL RIGHT! ATTA BOY, NAKAYA!
NOW YOU JUST GOTTA WORK ON PASSING.
YOU'RE REALLY GUNG-HO OUT THERE TODAY.
HUH?
I'M ALWAYS GUNG-HO.

OOH! YEAH?
MIYUKI-CHAN.
HM?
JOUSEI.
WHY YOU GOTTA YANK ME AROUND LIKE THAT?!
WHAT GIVES?!
NOTHING.
......
Until now, we always did everything together...
Feeling sorta lonesome.
NAKAYA!
Yank you around...
Get over 'ere.
RIGHT!

OH.
NAKAYA?
OH, HEY, SHINO. YOU AT WORK?
UH...
YEAH.
IT'S OKAY IF YOU'RE HOME LATE.
I'LL BE A GOOD BOY AND JUST EAT AND GO TO BED.
AND... MAYBE I'LL POP IN A FEW OF YOUR CDS, TOO...
HUH?!
NOT.
HA HA HA!
......
BY THE WAY, NAKAYA...
UH... TODAY...YOU DIDN'T GET HURT, OR ANYTHING, DID YOU?
HURT? HELL YEAH.
BUT JUST SCRATCHES.
IS THAT SO...?

THANK GOODNESS...
AS LONG AS IT'S NOTHING SERIOUS...
OH.
MIZUSAWA-KUN...
GOOD WORK TODAY, HISAE-SAN.
WHAT'RE YOU STILL DOING HERE?
I WAS WAITING FOR YOU.
I WAS HOPING I COULD TALK TO YOU ABOUT SOMETHING...

HE NEEDS ADVICE?
So do I...
SURE, IF I CAN BE OF HELP...
OH... PLEASE FEEL FREE TO SIT WHEREVER.
HUH? OH, YES.
I'M ALWAYS SO NERVOUS AT OTHER PEOPLE'S HOUSES...
GOOD ANSWER.
PFFT!

THAT'S RIGHT...LAST TIME WAS AT TENRYU-SAN'S PLACE.
I WAS DRUNK AND...
...STAYED UNTIL MORNING...
HUH?
THAT REMINDS ME... MIZUSAWA-KUN...
...WAS SHACKED UP WITH SOME GUY!!
IS THERE SOMETHING THE MATTER?
I HOPE GINGER ALE IS OKAY?

OH!
YES!
YOUR VOICE ...
Heh Heh
...GIVES YOU AWAY.
WHAT WAS IT YOU WANTED TO TALK TO ME ABOUT?
THERE ISN'T ANY-THING.
WELL THEN...

UM...?
I SWEAR.
YOU ARE ABSOLUTELY ADORABLE, HISAE-SAN.
NOT JUST YOUR VOICE...
YOU TWO'VE BEEN PAIRED UP A LOT RECENTLY, HAVEN'T YOU?
...BUT ALL OF YOU.
I LIKE HEARING YOUR VOICE.
WHOA! WAIT...WAIT A MINUTE!
THE TRUTH IS I'VE BEEN WAITING FOR A CHANCE LIKE THIS...

HISAE-SAN...
TENRYU-SAN!
HISAE-SAN...
JUST HOW FAR HAVE YOU GONE WITH TENRYU-SAN?
SEEMS LIKE YOU'VE GOTTEN A FEW KISSES IN, AT LEAST.

NO!
WE HAVE DONE NO SUCH THING!
URK!
DEAD WHITE!
WELL, THEN I GET TO BE YOUR FIRST.
YOUR SON'S ALWAYS THROWING ME DIRTY LOOKS...
...SO I WAS GETTING WORRIED I'D NEVER GET ANYWHERE WITH YOU, HISAE-SAN.

AH!
LUCKY ME.
MIZUSAWA-KUN! THIS ISN'T FUNNY...!
L-LET ME GO!
TRY TO PUSH ME AWAY.
I CERTAINLY WOULDN'T MIND THAT.
UNH...
NNGH...!
THIS IS WRONG...!

... FORGIVE ME...
PLEASE DON'T SULLY OUR WORK!
HISAE-SAN.

I...
I'M THE TYPE WHO REALLY GETS INTO HIS ROLE.
IT WASN'T MY INTENT TO TOY WITH YOU...
...SO PLEASE DON'T HATE ME.
FINE...
I LIKE YOU.
ガコー

I'M HOME...
What a day...
WELCOME BACK.
OH, YOU'RE STILL UP, NAKAYA?
YEAH...
I GOTTA TALK TO YOU.
I'VE BEEN THINKING ...
...ABOUT TRANSFERRING TO JOUSEI HIGH SCHOOL.

HUH?
SO YOU'RE GOING TO START SERIOUSLY FOCUSING ON HOCKEY?
YEP.
THAT'S MY PLAN AT LEAST.
BUT... KUNIWAKI-KUN SAID...
WHAT?
WHAT DID HE SAY?
WHAT?!
HE SAID I HAVEN'T BEEN PAYING ATTENTION TO HOCKEY?! WHERE THE HELL DID HE GET THAT?!

YEAH...
AND HE TOLD ME YOU COULD GET SERIOUSLY INJURED.
THAT JACKASS!
HE IS SO DEAD!
WAIT, NAKAYA!
THAT TRUTH IS... I'VE BEEN WORRIED ABOUT YOU TOO.
YOU WERE ALWAYS SO INTENSE ABOUT YOUR HOCKEY, BUT WHEN YOU SUDDENLY GOT INTO THAT ANIME...
WELL, I MEAN IT MAKES ME HAPPY TO SEE YOU INTERESTED IN MY VOICE ACTING JOBS, BUT...

...I STARTED TO FEEL THAT THAT WASN'T THE REAL YOU.
WHAT'RE YOU TALKING ABOUT?!
WHAT'S SO WRONG ABOUT ME WATCHING ANIME?!
B-BUT...
It's supposed to be for kids...
I JUST LIKE IT! AND ANYWAY, I'M STILL A KID!!
Hey! No crying!
I JUST DIDN'T KNOW WHAT I'D DO IF YOU QUIT HOCKEY...

I CAN'T BELIEVE THIS!
I THOUGHT YOU HATED ME DOING HOCKEY!
I DO, BUT...
I'M SORRY...

IT'S NOT YOUR FAULT.
AFTER ALL, YOU'RE NEW AT THIS PARENTING STUFF...
BUT YOU KNOW, I'M NOT THE KIND OF GUY WHO JUST COMPLETELY CHANGES WHAT HE CARES ABOUT ON A WHIM.
SO REMEMBER THAT, PLEASE. OKAY, SHINO?
OKAY...
I'LL KEEP THAT IN MIND.

OH, BY THE WAY. A FAX CAME IN FOR YOU FROM THE OFFICE.
IT'S ABOUT YOUR RADIO SHOW GIG.
I SEE...
TENRYU-SAN'LL BE ON THE SHOW TOO, RIGHT?
OH THAT'S RIGHT. WE'RE DOING IT TOGETHER.
I HAVEN'T SEEN HIM IN FOREVER. CAN I COME ALONG TOO? IT'S SUNDAY AND ALL.
FINE WITH ME.
THAT'S RIGHT... NOW WHO WAS THE HOST FOR THIS AGAIN?

TENRYU-SAN.
YO.
HELLO.
HEY THERE, SON.
SO I HEAR YOU'RE A BIG FAN OF "MIRACLE DIETER."
YEAH! TOTALLY.
SHINO WAS WORRIED ABOUT YOU. YOU SHOULD'VE SEEN HIM GETTING ALL WEEPY AT THE BAR THE OTHER NIGHT.
HA HA!
Ouch.
TENRYU-SAN...

GOOD MORNING!
HEY!
HUH?
OH DON'T TELL ME YOU FORGOT.
THIS IS MY SHOW, HISAE-SAN.
WHAT?
SERIOUSLY...?

ON
STUDIO
WELCOME TO MIZUSAWA TERUSHI'S "FAST BREAK"!
TODAY WE HAVE MY OH-SO-LOVELY COUPLING PARTNER, HISAE SHINO.
AND MY EVER-GRAND SENPAI, KOIZUMI TENRYU.
LOVELY COUPLING PARTNER, EH?
DON'T ASK...
NOW JUST WHAT ARE YOU TWO MUTTERING ABOUT?
YOU KNOW, SPEAKING FOR MYSELF, I ABSOLUTEL
ADORE HISAE-SAN'S VOICE.
TENRYU-SAN, YOU'VE BEEN TOGETHER WITH HISAE-SAN FOR A WHILE NOW, RIGHT?
WHAT DO YOU MEAN BY "TOGETHER"?
That's right.
I almost forgot how those two can be.
SOUTH POLE
OH YOU KNOW, THE USUAL.
UH, EXCUSE ME.
MIZUSAWA-KUN? ENOUGH WITH THE SUGGESTIVE REMARKS.

HUH?
I WASN'T SUGGESTING ANYTHING.
...
OH GOD... I JUST WANT TO GET OUT OF HERE.
AS SOON AS POSSIBLE...
IF I REMEMBER CORRECTLY, WE MET DURING SHINO'S DEBUT SERIES.
YEAH, AT THAT TIME...
SEE? THAT COUNTS AS BEING TOGETHER FOR A LONG TIME INDEED!
AND I'M KIND OF A MORE RECENT THING, AREN'T I, HISAE-SAN?
AND WHAT'S THAT SUPPOSED TO MEAN?

UWAAH... NAKAYA'S MAKING THAT SCARY FACE AGAIN.
SH...SHALL WE CHANGE THE TOPIC?
AND JUST WHEN HE WAS REALLY STARTING TO SHOW INTEREST IN MY VOICE ACTING CAREER...
OKAY THEN.
IT'S NOT LIKE WE'RE FOLLOWING A SCRIPT OR ANYTHING.
YOU KNOW, HISAE-SAN, I HAVEN'T HAD TOO MANY OPPORTUNITIES TO COUPLE WITH YOU YET, BUT...
PLEASE, DON'T GO THERE...
I REALLY MUST SAY YOU ARE QUITE TALENTED.
T-TALENTED?

YOU KNOW, LIKE YOUR KISSING SCENES.
M-MIZUSAWA-KUN?!
IS SOMETHING THE MATTER?
ARE WE...
...
ARE WE BROADCASTING LIVE?
THAT'S CORRECT!
I HOPE ALL YOU LISTENERS AT HOME HAVE ENJOYED THE PROCEEDINGS SO FAR!
No...it's nothing.
sniff
WHAT'S WRONG?

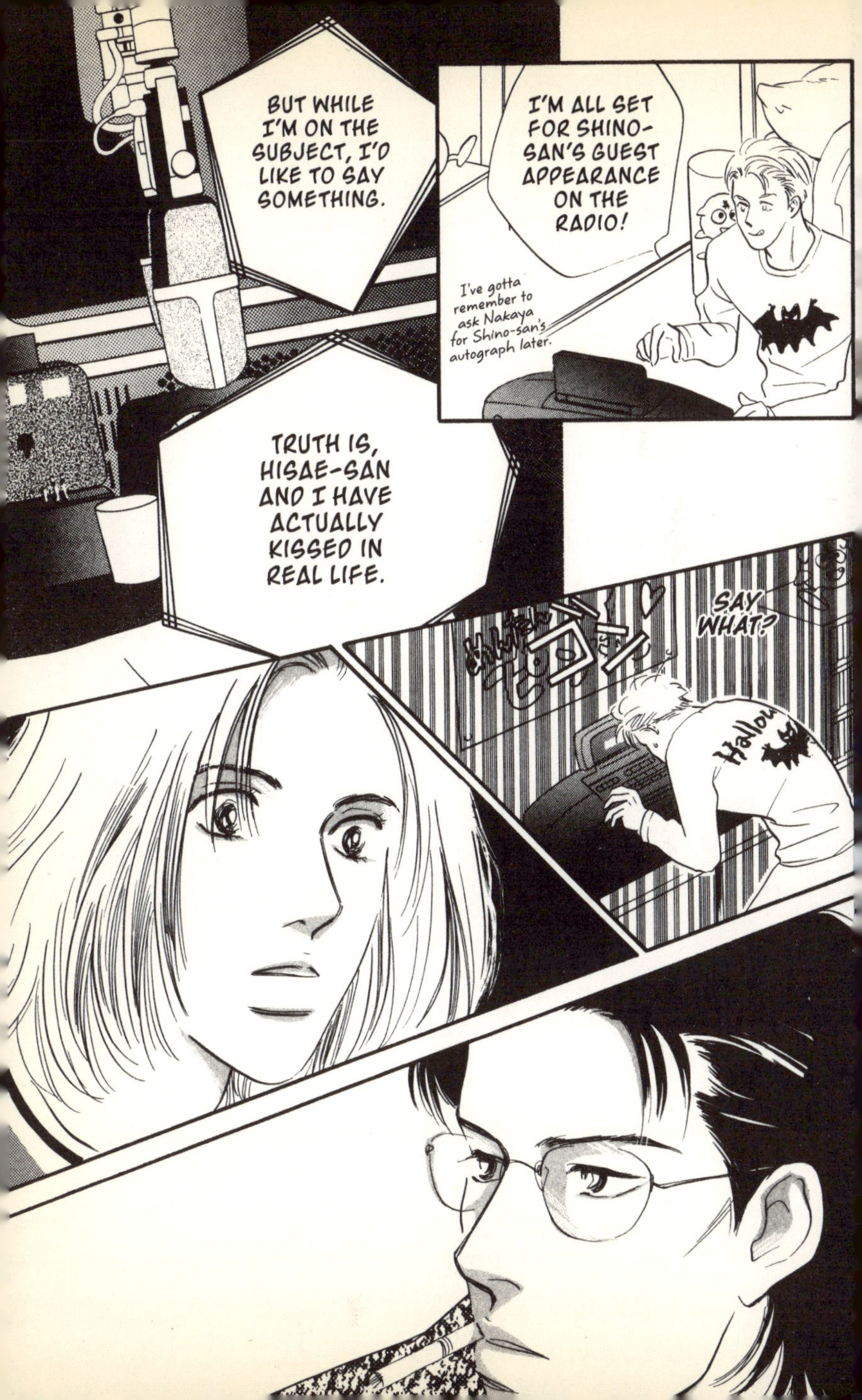
I'M ALL SET FOR SHINO-SAN'S GUEST APPEARANCE ON THE RADIO!
I've gotta remember to ask Nakaya for Shino-san's autograph later.
BUT WHILE I'M ON THE SUBJECT, I'D LIKE TO SAY SOMETHING.
TRUTH IS, HISAE-SAN AND I HAVE ACTUALLY KISSED IN REAL LIFE.
SAY WHAT?
Hallow

IT WAS HIS FIRST KISS!
DENY IT!!
DAMN IT, SHINO!!
WRONG.

THAT WASN'T HIS FIRST KISS.
HUH?
Huh?
I WAS SHINO'S FIRST KISS.
HUH?

HUH?!
WHEN'D YOU DO IT, TENRYU-SAN?!
Dammit, I knew it!
HMM...
WHEN WAS IT HE SPENT THE NIGHT THAT ONE TIME...?
HISAE-SAN, IS THAT TRUE?
I...I...

SHINO!
STOP...
TELL 'EM, SHINO.
OH, THAT'S RIGHT.
THAT ONE TIME...
YOU GOT COMPLETELY PLASTERED AND PASSED OUT, RIGHT?
STOP IT...
WHAT?!
DID THAT REALLY HAPPEN, HISAE-SAN?!
Right?
IT... CAN'T BE...

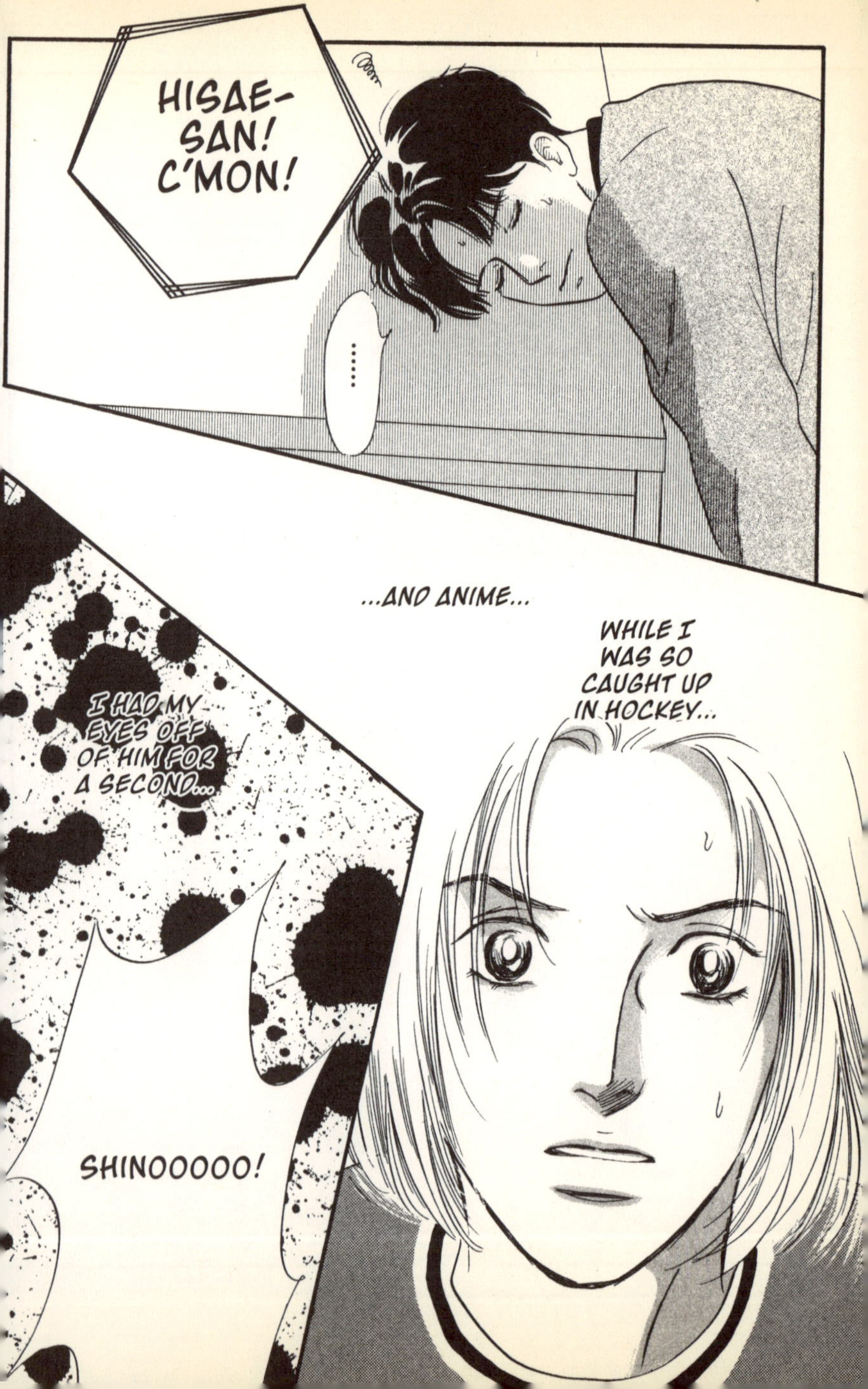
HISAE-SAN! C'MON!
......
WHILE I WAS SO CAUGHT UP IN HOCKEY...
...AND ANIME...
I HAD MY EYES OFF OF HIM FOR A SECOND...
SHINOOOOO!

HISAE-SAN!
SAY IT AIN'T SO!
I'M SORRY.
NAKAYA.
I'M SORRY I'M SUCH A FAILURE OF A FATHER.
WHAT'RE YOU GETTING SO WORKED UP ABOUT?
SO BETWEEN TENRYU AND ME, WHO'S THE BETTER KISSER?
......
Merciless!

MEAN-WHILE, KUNIWAKI IS...
DANG.
MISSED AGAIN.
ウイィィ・・・・ン
NOT ANOTHER "DEMON GLUTTON Z."
MIYUKI'S THE ONLY ONE THAT NAKAYA WOULD REALLY WANT.
I should've just bought one at the start...

#4 END

SHOUT OUT LOUD!™
#5

MY DAD, HISAE SHINO, IS A VOICE ACTOR.
AND I'M YOUR AVERAGE GUY IN HIGH SCHOOL.
IT'S ONLY RECENTLY THAT I'VE COME TO TERMS WITH MY DAD'S PROFES-SION...
...BUT...
...FOR SHINO, WHOSE VOICE AND FACE BELIE HIS AGE, THIS JOB IS JUST ONE DANGER AFTER ANOTHER!

Industrial Bank Lease
VOICE-M Planning
#1 Corporation
AN AUDITION?
So you mean...
IT'S NOT YAOI, IS IT?
OOH, SHINO DEAR, YOU'RE NOT GETTING ALL SELF-CONSCIOUS ON ME NOW, ARE YOU?
WH-WHAT DO YOU MEAN SELF-CONSCIOUS?
About what?
B-BUT THERE'S ...
I DIDN'T MEAN IT LIKE THAT...
OH, NO! I'M JUST SO PROUD OF YOU!
I SEE YOU'RE FINALLY GROWING UP AND BECOMING AN ADULT!
HOW SHALL I PUT IT... SUCH A RUSH OF EMOTIONS FLOWING THROUGH MY HEART!
Why are you always so weird?

BUT ANYWAY, IT'S NOT YAOI.
ALAS.
BUT IF YOU REALLY WANT TO DO ONE, I CAN PULL SOME STRINGS FOR YOU.
NO THANKS!
WHAT'S THAT YOU SAY?!
TSU-TSUKA-CHAN! TSUKAMOTO-SAN! JUST TELL ME WHAT THE AUDITION IS!
IT'S A VIDEO ANIME SERIES BASED OFF OF A NOVEL.
THERE WILL BE THREE SEASONS, COMPRISED OF A TOTAL OF SEVENTY-SIX THIRTY-MINUTE EPISODES. IT'S A PRETTY LENGTHY SERIES!
THAT REALLY IS SOMETHING.
THE TEN MAIN CHARACTERS WILL BE SELECTED BASED ON YOUR AUDITIONS...
...ON THIS DAY AT THIS TIME.
SEVENTY-SIX EPISODES ...
UM...
BY THE WAY, WHAT KIND OF STORY IS IT?

IN ONE WORD, IT'S A WAR EPIC.
OH...LIKE GUNDAM?
YEAH, COULD BE.
WILL ALL TEN CHARACTERS GET TO TRANSFORM AND STUFF?
WHAT'RE YOU BABBLING ABOUT?
WELL... I MEAN, IT SEEMS KIND OF CHILDISH.
YOU FOOL!!
"Childish"?! You're childish!
I SAID IT WAS BASED ON A NOVEL, REMEMBER?!
You think something "childish" can last 76 episodes?!
THE COMPLETE 21-VOLUME MASTERPIECE: GALACTIC LEGEND OF THE THREE KINGDOMS.
FAR OFF, ON THE OUTSKIRTS OF THE GALAXY...
... THREE HEROES HOLD THE FATE OF THE EMPIRE IN THEIR VERY HANDS IN THIS MAGNIFICENT SAGA!
BEHOLD !!

UH...
Where'd that costume come from?
BE AWED! THE ONSLAUGHT OF YAOI FAN BOOKS!!
REAL
Preparatory Volume
BAD 1/2
NEVER UNDER-ESTIMATE THE OTAKU SUPPORT!!
GAH!
UH... TSUKAMOTO-SAN...? WHICH...WHICH CHARACTER WILL I PLAY...?
My goodness!
YOU'RE THE LIKELY CANDIDATE FOR THIS GUY HERE.
Character
Crystal Lone (Age 13) Version (1) (in civilian attire)
* Hair has highlights
Eye
CRYSTAL LONE. AGE 13.

A FACTION OF THE SPACE ARMY HAS GAINED INDEPENDENCE FROM THE EMPIRE.
THE REVERED YOUNG GENERAL WHO WOULD LEAD THEM IS A WAR ORPHAN FROM A CHILDREN'S SCHOOL.
BUT WHAT IS WORTHY OF SPECIAL MENTION IS HIS INTELLECT AND FLASH OF GENIUS THINKING THAT SETS HIM ABOVE THE REST.
I THINK THIS WOULD BE MY FIRST TIME PLAYING SUCH A... DRAMATIC ROLE.
HEY, I'M HOME.
OH... WELCOME BACK, NAKAYA.
HUH. AREN'T YOU HOME EARLY TODAY?
WAIT A MINUTE.
THIS IS GALACTIC LEGEND OF THE THREE KINGDOMS, RIGHT?
Galactic Legend of the Three Kingdoms
OH, YOU KNOW IT?
FILA

YEAH.
WHAT, YOU GUYS MAKING THIS INTO A CD TOO?
NO...AN ANIME...
WHICH CHARACTER WILL YOU BE?
WELL, THEY HAVEN'T HELD THE AUDITION YET, BUT...
I'LL PROBABLY BE CRYSTAL LONE.
CRYS...
YOU MEAN...
THE LITTLE BRAT?
YEAH, WHAT'S WRONG WITH THAT?
...
I DUNNO, IT JUST DOESN'T SUIT YOU.
IF SHINO'S GOING TO BE IN THIS...
...HE'D BE MUCH BETTER AS...
FILA SPORT

......
SHINO!
ビクゥ
CRASH
ARE THOSE OTHER GUYS GONNA TRY OUT TOO?!
TH...
THOSE OTHER GUYS...?
KOIZUMI TENRYU AND MIZUSAWA TERUSHI!
I...
I DON'T KNOW...

I KNEW IT...
THIS IS GOING TO REQUIRE SPECIAL ATTENTION.
AFTER ALL...
WITH THOSE TWO AROUND, THERE'S NO WAY I CAN RELAX AND KEEP MY MIND ON HOCKEY.
IT'S THEIR FAULT!
I WAS SHINO'S FIRST KISS.
GRRR! GRRR!
IT WAS HIS FIRST KISS!
KISS... KISS...
You don't do that to someone's dad!
HOW DARE THEY KISS HIM!
KEEP THE DIRTY BEHAVIOR...
CRASH
BOOM
BASH
...IN THE STUDIO, THANK YOU VERY MUCH!!
Eep!

LISTEN, NAKAYA...
DON'T YOU HAVE... SCHOOL, OR SOMETHING?
YEAH?
WHAT ABOUT IT?
YO, NAKAYA.
Mornin'.
WHEW! KUNIWAKI-KUN!
WHISPER
W...WELL, I'LL BE GOING TO WORK NOW!
SHINO!!
HEY...! WAIT A MINUTE, SHINO!

I'M GOING TO YOUR AUDITION, TOO!!
You've got class, buddy.
STOP WORRYING SO MUCH!
I'M NOT A CHILD!
YOU SAYIN' YOU'RE AN ADULT?!
So he finally crossed that line.
AT ANY RATE...
YOU WILL ONLY BE ENROLLED AT THIS SCHOOL UNTIL THE END OF THE SCHOOL YEAR.
AND THEN YOUR PLANS ARE TO APPLY TO JOUSEI HIGH SCHOOL.
OI!
ARE YOU LISTENING TO ME AT ALL, NAKAYA?
I'M LISTENING, I'M LISTENING.

YOU KNOW...
...AT THIS RATE, WILL SHINO'S VIRTUE BE SAFE?
YAMABE!!
WELL...I WAS LISTENING TO THAT RADIO SHOW A FEW DAYS AGO...
I'M JUST WORRIED, THAT'S ALL.
WHAT KIND OF HOMEROOM TEACHER WORRIES ABOUT THE VIRTUE OF HIS STUDENT'S DAD?!
MY KIND.
WELL, YOU SEE...
I'M A GENUINE FAN OF HISAE SHINO AS A VOICE ACTOR.
AND WHEN YOU CHANGE SCHOOLS ...
...I'LL BE FREE TO PURSUE HIM MYSELF!
SO HURRY UP AND GET OUT, NAKAYA!
...
Pursue him...?!
I've been a good and prudent homeroom teacher long enough!

Dammit! How come I'm not allowed to punch him?
HEY...
YOU EVER CONSIDER NOT OBSESSING ABOUT YOUR POP FOR A WHILE?
SHUT UP.
......
Goddammit!
OGAWA
WHY'S HE ALWAYS GOTTA PUT HIMSELF IN SITUATIONS LIKE THIS?
I BETTER KEEP A CLOSER EYE ON HIM...

I MEAN...
I KNOW HE'S AN ADULT AND ALL, BUT...
IF I DON'T KEEP A LEVEL HEAD...
...WHO KNOWS WHAT MIGHT HAPPEN NEXT TIME?
コン
WHAT THE HELL?! THAT WAS MY PUCK!
KEEP SPACING OUT LIKE THAT, AND YOU'RE GONNA END UP ON YOUR ASS.

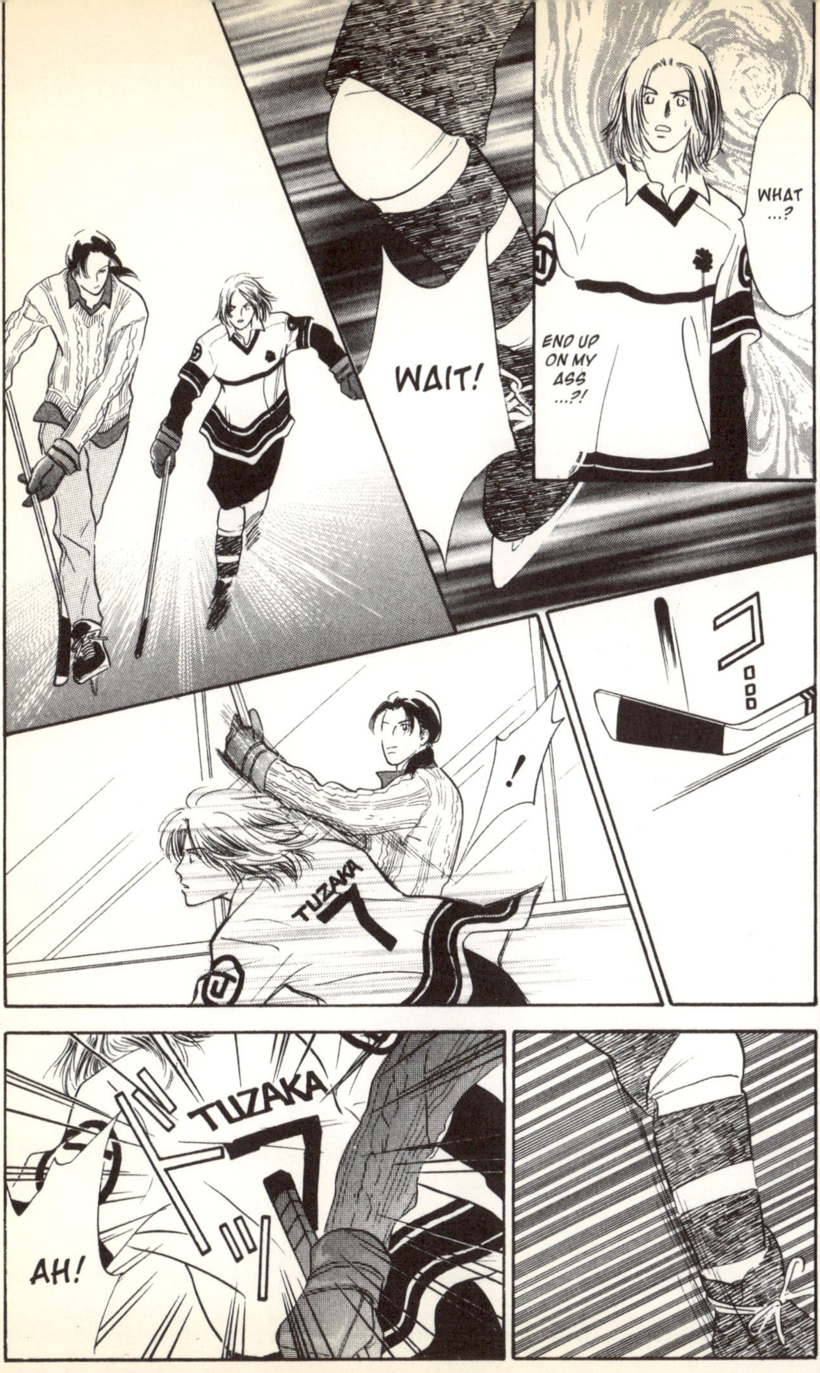
WHAT ...?
END UP ON MY ASS ...?!
WAIT!
?...
!
TUZAKA 7
TUZAKA 7
AH!

FUSE!
QUIT PLAYIN' AROUND!
WE'VE GOT A HIGH BIDDER ON NAKAYA THERE!
GOTCHA.
FUSE...?
YOU'RE GOING TO JOUSEI, EH?
I GUESS A CORPORATION DEAL SOUNDS MORE GLORIOUS THAN COLLEGE LEAGUE.

DON'T MISTAKE POWER FOR SKILL.
KEEP THAT SLENDER FIGURE OF YOURS.
WHAT THE?!
YOU OKAY THERE?
JUST WHO THE HECK IS THAT... THAT...?!
THAT'S FUSE AKIHI. HE'S THE COACH OF THE JUNIOR TEAM.
CO...
COACH?
SEEMS HE WAS SIGNED WITH THE CANADIAN NATIONAL TEAM.
IN THAT CASE...
...WHAT'S HE DOING HERE? HE'S TOO YOUNG TO HAVE RETIRED.
THEY SAY HE BUSTED HIS KNEE.
SO HE'S IN NO POSITION TO HANDLE THE BIG LEAGUES ANYMORE.

HIS... KNEE?
IF I KEEP THIS UP...
...THERE'S NO DOUBT THAT NAKAYA WILL BE CONCERNED.
BUT... THERE'S NOTHING I CAN DO ABOUT THAT.
I MEAN, IT'S NOT LIKE I'M JUST TRYING OUT FOR THIS PART...
...IN ORDER TO SET MYSELF UP TO BE TAKEN ADVANTAGE OF.
SO WHAT'S THE PROBLEM?
GOOD MORNING!

WHOA...
THERE ARE SO MANY CANDIDATES.
HERE HE IS!
YO!
CALL HIM!
ERR...
CALL MIZUSAWA!
DON'T TELL ME...
OH!
HISAE-SAN!
MI...
MORNIN'.

I FIGURED YOU'D BE HERE TOO.
!
TENRYU-SAN.
Didn't sleep much last night, and I'm in a bad mood.
YOU "FIGURED"?
YOUR POINT?
SO, WHAT'S ALL THE FUSS ABOUT?
TENRYU-CHAN!
SHAME ON YOU, MAKING A MOVE ON HIM LIKE THAT!
Do you two really have that kind of relationship?
THAT KISS, SILLY!
I heard it on the radio.
OH, RIGHT.
THAT?
YOU KNOW YOU CAN'T WIN, WHATEVER YOU DO.
NOT WITH MIZUSAWA AS YOUR OPPONENT!
Ha ha ha...
BUT WASN'T THAT ALL JUST A JOKE?
IT WAS SCRIPTED.
RIGHT?
WHAT WAS?
......
I'M GLAD WE'LL BE TOGETHER AGAIN, HISAE-SAN.

HUH?
UM...
HE WAS... TOTALLY GLARING AT ME...
What gives?
YO, SHINO.
UWAH!
SHINO?
UH...UM, PARDON ME!
WHAT'RE YOU APOLOGIZING FOR?

NO, IT'S JUST...
IT SEEMS EVERYONE'S GOING OVERBOARD ABOUT THAT JOKE YOU MADE.
JOKE?
WELL, ANYWAY MIZUSAWA-KUN--
WAIT, SHINO.
WHAT DO YOU MEAN "JOKE"?
WELL...THE ONE YOU SAID ON THE RADIO SHOW...
ABOUT THE KISS?
YEAH...
DID YOU REALLY KISS MIZUSAWA?
UH...UH, THAT IS... UM...
ギクッ
OKAY, WE'RE GOING TO BEGIN NOW!

Y- YESSIR.
......
ザワ
ザワ

OH...
MIZUSAWA AND THIS CHARACTER MATCH PERFECTLY.
AND TENRYU-SAN TOO... HE'D DEFINITELY BE THE BEST FOR THIS ONE.
IT JUST DOESN'T SUIT YOU.
HMM...

OKAY THEN.
NEXT WE'LL BE HAVING CRYSTAL LONE TRY-OUTS.
HISAE-KUN.
KATORI-KUN. IF YOU PLEASE.
YES.
YES.
OH...IT'S THAT GUY FROM BEFORE.
MY NAME IS KATORI KOUSUKE.
"WELL, WHAT DO YOU THINK ABOUT IT, ADMIRAL?"
"MY HEART... ACHES...AT THE THOUGHT OF THE CAPTAIN'S DEATH..."
"IT WILL TAKE SOME TIME..."

THIS IS...
...HIS ROLE!
OH... SHINO.
HEY... TENRYU-SAN...
WHAT'S THE MATTER?
YOU DON'T LOOK VERY HAPPY.
I GUESS...

HIROSE-SAN.
TOKITOU-SAN. CAN YOU PLEASE COME IN HERE AGAIN?
RIGHT.
COMING.
THAT KATORI-KUN IS PRETTY TALENTED.
YEAH. HE AND I COME FROM THE SAME AGENCY.
HE'S YOUNG BUT HE'S DEFINITELY GIFTED.
HE'S ALREADY GOT THE AIR OF A MAJOR LEAGUE VOICE ACTOR.
HUH ...
IS THAT SO?
UM, HISAE-SAN?
IF YOU WOULD DO ONE MORE ROUND FOR US?
HUH?
OH, OF COURSE.
HISAE-KUN. THIS TIME...
...WE WANT YOU TO TRY DOING "JOHN ADERETTE."

JOHN ADERETTE...
HE'S ONE OF THE TRIO OF HEROES.
IF I REMEMBER CORRECTLY, HE'S THE RESOURCEFUL YET ABSENT-MINDED GENERAL...
A 30-YEAR-OLD BACHELOR WITH A BABY-FACE?!
SOUNDS PERFECT.
I DON'T CARE EITHER WAY, BUT...
IF HISAE-SAN GETS CAST, THE IDEA OF WORKING SIDE-BY-SIDE FOR SO LONG MAKES ME UNCOMFORTABLE.
AND WHY IS THAT?
WELL, BECAUSE YOU'LL BE HERE TOO, TENRYU-SAN.
YOU CAN'T...
...SAY THAT FOR SURE JUST YET.

I SUPPOSE.
I'M HOME!
NAKAYA?
HEY.

UH-HUH ...
YOU'RE WATCHING A VIDEO?
......
Lease
VOICE:M Planning
#1 Corporation
SHINO, THEY DECIDED!

OH...YOU MEAN ABOUT THE AUDITION, TSUKAMOTO-SAN?
THAT'S RIGHT!
THIS CASTING REALLY EXCEEDED MY EXPECTATIONS!
Crystal Lone--Katori Kousuke
OH...
John Aderette--Hisae Shino
Prince Akbar--Mizusawa Terushi
Tokio Isfahan--Koizumi Tenryu
HUH?
NO WAY...
YOU GOT A LEADING ROLE! A MAIN CHARACTER!
BANZAI!
OH...
I'M SO HAPPY...
THIS IS AMAZING!
I KNEW ALL ALONG THAT CRYSTAL WASN'T RIGHT FOR ME.

NOW, GO FORTH AND WORK WITH ALL YOUR MIGHT!
YES SIR!
NEXT TIME, HOW ABOUT A SHOTA PIECE?
A 15 YEAR-OLD.
It starts off with a rape by a stepbrother. He's a "might makes right" kinda guy.
You can do it, right? Right? Right??
M-might makes... right...?
...
I SHOULD TELL NAKAYA AS SOON AS POSSIBLE.
NOW WE'RE GOING TO DO THE MONOLOGUE FROM THE MIDDLE OF SCENE 19.
IF WE COULD HAVE HISAE-KUN BY HIMSELF?
YES.
AND FOR THE NEXT SCENE...
WE'RE GOING TO HAVE TO DO ANOTHER TAKE. WE GOT A LITTLE TOO MUCH NOISE IN THE BACKGROUND.
Sorry about that!
GOOD NIGHT!
AWW, IT'S RAINING.
SHINO-SAN, WHAT'RE YOU GOING TO DO?
HUH...

ザァ…
TENRYU-SAN'S PLACE ISN'T TOO FAR FROM HERE.
I'VE GOT SOMEWHERE TO BE, SO GO ON AHEAD WITHOUT ME.
Oh, really?
バシャ
バシャ
THIS IS SO STRANGE...
YOU GOT COMPLETELY PLASTERED AND PASSED OUT.
I WAS DEAD DRUNK SO I DON'T REMEMBER MUCH ABOUT THAT NIGHT.
I SHOULD LEAVE. DROPPING BY OUT OF THE BLUE LIKE THIS... I'LL JUST BE BOTHERING HIM, I'M SURE.
カァ…

WHAT'RE YOU DOING HERE, SHINO?
TE...
TENRYU-SAN!
ER...
WELL, YOU SEE.
WORK RAN OVER.
AND I REMEMBERED THAT YOU DIDN'T LIVE TOO FAR FROM THE STUDIO...
ALTHOUGH I ACTUALLY HAD A HARD TIME RECALLING EXACTLY WHERE.
UNDERSTANDABLE.
AFTER ALL, YOU WERE INEBRIATED THE LAST TIME YOU WERE HERE.

HOW ABOUT A SHOWER?
AND A CHANGE OF CLOTHES?
OH... IT'S OKAY.
I SHOULD BE HEADED HOME SOON.
RIGHT...
!
SHIIIIINO...
WERE YOU AWAKE?

A-AWAKE ...?
I DON'T KNOW WHAT YOU'RE TALKING ABOUT.
COME OFF IT. WHEN YOU KISSED MIZUSAWA.
THAT HAS NOTHING TO DO WITH THIS...
I WASN'T JOKING BACK THEN.
I REALLY DID KISS YOU.
I SAID AS MUCH, DIDN'T I? BUT YOU WERE PRETTY OUT OF IT.
I....
I GOT A GOOD THIRTY SECONDS OF KISS.

TE...
WH...
WHY...
BECAUSE I WANTED TO.
DOESN'T IT...
DOESN'T IT FEEL STRANGE TO DO THAT?

NN.
YOU DON'T LIKE IT?
PLEASE...
PLEASE DON'T ASK ME THINGS I CAN'T ANSWER...
TE...
MMM...
SEE? IT DOESN'T FEEL STRANGE AT ALL.
HOLD ON...!

SLIDE
AH!
OW... OW OW OW...
YOU OKAY?
IF YOU'RE JUST TEASING ME, PLEASE STOP.
TENRYU-SAN.
I...
I'M ALREADY SUCH A POOR EXCUSE FOR FATHER, I DON'T NEED TO MAKE THINGS WORSE...

MY APOLOGIES, SHINO.
BUT NO MATTER WHAT YOU THINK ABOUT YOURSELF AS A FATHER...
...I THINK YOU MAKE A FINE ONE.
IT'S JUST...
I'VE FALLEN FOR YOU.
AND MIZUSAWA MAY HAVE, TOO.
TEN... RYU-SAN...
DID KISSING ME...
...FEEL STRANGE TO YOU?

HUH?
N-NO... NOT REALLY...
I SEE, THEN!
UM...?

BE CAREFUL ON YOUR WAY BACK HOME, SHINO!
JUST IGNORE IT IF ANY SHADY OLD MEN TRY TO TALK TO YOU!
I WONDER IF HE'S DONE THIS JOB SO MUCH THAT HE'S GOTTEN A LITTLE TOO USED TO THIS SORT OF THING?
Although I don't think it's quite that...
TENRYU-SAN... WE'LL BE TOGETHER ON THIS NEXT OAV PROJECT, RIGHT?

YEP...
WELL...
SEE YOU.
HUH...? IT'S HIM...

KATORI-KUN?
HE AND I COME FROM THE SAME AGENCY.

EXIT
SPORT
DON'T YOU EVER GET TO GO OUT ON THE ICE?

IF MY OPPONENT'S AT YOUR LEVEL, THEN I'D BE OKAY.
GRR
FILA SPORT
THEN LET'S DO IT!
AND THIS TIME WON'T BE ANYTHING LIKE THE LAST ONE!

WHAT THE HELL IS FUSE UP TO?

!
SHIT!
GET BACK HERE!

YOU'RE TEN YEARS AHEAD OF YOURSELF, BOY.
DAMMIT!
HUFF
HUFF
HUFF
NO WONDER HE WAS ON THE NATIONAL TEAM.
カチャ
LA SPORT

OH...
I...

DON'T JUST STAND THERE.
COME ON IN.
SO...
DOES YOUR KNEE HURT? I THOUGHT IT WOULD...
OH...
THIS?
YEAH, ONCE IN A WHILE.
GOING UP AGAINST A YOUNG THING LIKE YOU MAKES ME WANT TO GO ALL OUT.
LIAR!
YOU HELD BACK THE WHOLE TIME!

I'LL TAKE THAT AS A COMPLIMENT.
THANKS.
I...
I WANTED TO ASK YOU...
IF YOU WOULDN'T JUST COACH THE JUNIOR TEAM...
...BUT BE MY PERSONAL COACH, TOO.
ME...?

FIRST, BUILD UP THAT BODY OF YOURS.
OR OPPONENTS WILL JUST BLOW RIGHT THROUGH YOU.
COUGH COUGH HACK
I'LL SEE WHEN I HAVE FREE TIME.
IT'LL BE A GOOD CHANGE OF PACE.
ヒョコ

I'M HOME...
YOU'VE BEEN WATCHING THAT ONE VIDEO A LOT LATELY, HAVEN'T YOU NAKAYA?
THERE SOME PLAYER IN THERE YOU LIKE?
SOMY

YEAH!
THIS GUY HERE! HIS OFFENSE IS AMAZING!
IT'S HIS SLASH SHOOT.
SEE! HE JUST GOT IT IN!
ISN'T HE SOMETHING?!
WH...
WHAT IS IT?
OH.
NOTHING AT ALL...
SHINO ...
YOUR FACE IS RED.

……
YEAH... WELL, YOU'RE BLUSHING TOO...
...NAKAYA.
I AM NOT!
I'M JUST...
SAME HERE, THEN. IT'S JUST...
I'M NOT...
It's just...
#5 END

SHOUT OUT LOUD!™
#6

MY BLUE SKY
MY NAME'S HISAE NAKAYA. AGE 17, HIGH SCHOOL STUDENT.
MY DAD'S HISAE SHINO, A VOICE ACTOR.
WHEN I FIRST SAW SOME OF THESE CDS HE WORKS ON, I WAS BEYOND SHOCKED-- THE ROOM EVEN STARTED SPINNING AND STUFF.

WHO'D HAVE THOUGHT I'D END UP LISTENING TO THESE IN SECRET.
Shino'd flip if he knew.
BUT RECENTLY, I HAVEN'T BEEN FEELING QUITE NORMAL.
HISAE-SAN, YOU'RE...33, RIGHT?
THAT'S RIGHT.
AND, YOU, KOIZUMI-SAN. YOU'RE 35, IF I'M NOT MISTAKEN.
AND? WHAT ABOUT IT?

I WAS JUST THINKING THAT IT'S HARD TO BELIEVE YOU'RE ONLY TWO YEARS APART.
UNFORTUNATELY, IT SEEMS THAT HISAE-SAN ISN'T INTERESTED IN ANYONE YOUNGER THAN HIMSELF.
MI-MIZUSAWA-KUN?!
ビクッ
NO NEED TO GET JEALOUS.
NOW NOW... AS SWEET AS HISAE-SAN IS, RESTRAIN YOURSELVES!
HA HA HA!
S... sweet?
UH... UM...
BUT IT'S THE TRUTH!
HE ALWAYS MAKES ME FEEL LIKE I'M JUST IN THE WAY.
THAT'S BECAUSE YOU ARE.
HOW CAN YOU BE SO CRUEL, TENRYU-SAN?!
UM... WHAT WAS YOUR QUESTION ....?
Why does this always happen?
AH! YES, YES, THAT'S RIGHT! FORGIVE ME.
TODAY IS THE FIRST DAY OF RECORDING FOR THE OVA SERIES, "GALACTIC LEGEND OF THE THREE KINGDOMS."
AND YOU THREE ARE PLAYING OUR LEADING HEROES.

RECORDING HASN'T EVEN BEGUN YET AND I'M ALREADY EXHAUSTED.
GOOD MORNING.
HEY, KOUSUKE-KUN.
OH.
GOOD MORNING, MIZUSAWA-SAN.
LISTEN, YOU.
YOU'RE GONNA BE SPENDING A LOT OF TIME WITH HISAE-SAN.
DON'T EVEN THINK ABOUT SCREWING WITH HIM.
WHY ON EARTH WOULD I WANT TO MESS WITH HISAE-SAN?

......
I SEE NOW THAT TENRYU-SAN HAS TAUGHT YOU WELL.
THINK YOU'RE CUTE, DO YOU?
I CAN'T SAY I PARTICULARLY WANT YOU TO THINK I'M CUTE, MIZUSAWA-SAN.
SAY THAT AGAIN?
WHAT'RE YOU TWO GOING ON ABOUT?
MIZUSAWA-SAN'S PICKING ON ME.
OH, REALLY?
YES, REALLY.
I DON'T SEE WHAT'S SO WRONG WITH THAT. AFTER ALL, OUR CHARACTERS ARE MUTUAL ENEMIES.
YEAH, BUT I SURVIVE.
YOU AND HISAE-SAN BOTH GET KILLED OFF.
YEAH, WELL, TENRYU-SAN DIES FIRST!

HMPH.
I...
...HATE THAT GUY.
OH... GOOD MORNING.
KATORI-KUN.
...
GOOD MORNING ...
...
WHAT'S THE MATTER, SHINO?
I GET THE FEELING ...
...KATORI-KUN DOESN'T LIKE ME VERY MUCH.
He was scowling at me earlier...

* In cases where all the cells are not yet completed, a white screen is shown with a simple line running through it signifying the length of the dialogue.

WHAT DID I DO TO DESERVE THIS...?
KATORI-KUN AND I ARE GOING TO HAVE A LOT OF SCREEN-TIME TOGETHER.
NO...I DON'T KNOW WHAT'S GOING ON WITH HIM, BUT I CAN'T LET MY PERSONAL FEELINGS INTERFERE WITH MY WORK.
WHAT COULD I POSSIBLY HAVE DONE...
...TO MAKE KATORI-KUN DISLIKE ME?
YO!
YOU'RE LATE, NAKAYA.

UH HUH...
SHE SAID YOU'VE BEEN KINDA COLD TO HER LATELY.
OH...BY THE WAY, SOUKO'S BEEN LOOKING FOR YOU.
YAMABE NABBED ME JUST WHEN I WAS ON MY WAY OUT.
TOBZKI 95
YUSA 13
MIZUKI
YABANA 25
91
IITAKA 28

HEY, ISN'T THAT THE SENIOR TEAM?
WHAT'S FUSE-SAN DOING OUT ON THE ICE?!
ザッ
カッ
HEY!
SAME OLD TRICKS, EH?!

WAIT A SEC!
FUSE-SAN'S KNEE...!
CHILL OUT, NAKAYA. SEN-SAN AND ALL OF THOSE GUYS KNOW ABOUT IT.
CHECK HIM!
FUSE-SAN!

STOP PUSHING YOURSELF!
AND SEN-SAN! HOW IMMATURE!
DRAGGING HIM OUT TO DO THIS!
What's Nakaya up to?
Hey! What gives?!
Dragging him out? Where's your respect?!
NA--
NAKAYA.
YOU IDIOT!
ALL I DID WAS FALL!

WHAT'RE YOU GETTING SO WORKED UP OVER?!
B-BUT!
I JUST WANT TO BE ABLE TO SEE YOU AT YOUR BEST, FUSE-SAN!
BUT IF YOU PUSH YOURSELF TOO HARD, YOU MIGHT NEVER BE ABLE TO SKATE AGAIN! WOULDN'T THAT BE FAR WORSE?!
...
WH...
WHAT?
THAT'S NONE OF YOUR BUSINESS.
BUT STILL... THANKS.

YEAH...
ズキューン
...
FUSE
48
NAKAYA.
Hey!
SHUT UP!
トーン
トーン
PHEW...
I'M BEAT.
IF WE KEEP THIS PACE, HOW AM I EVER GOING TO SURVIVE DOING A WHOLE SERIES?

NAKAYA.
DINNER'S READY.
I'M NOT HUNGRY.
NAKAYA?
IS SOMETHING THE MATTER? DO YOU HAVE A COLD? OR A FEVER?
キィ
ビクッ
YOU DO HAVE A FEVER, DON'T YOU, NAKAYA?!
SHINO.
WHAT HAPPENED? LOOK, I'LL GO GET SOME MEDICINE...
I'M NOT SICK.

HUH?
I HAVE A QUESTION ...
WHEN YOU DO THAT KIND OF WORK...
"THAT KIND"?
THAT YAOI STUFF.
OH.
HA HA...
HOW DOES IT FEEL?
HUH?
I MEAN...
DIDN'T YOU HAVE TO EXPERIENCE HOW IT FEELS TO BE ABLE TO ACT IT?
Why is he asking this all of a sudden?
Especially something so personal.
...

HOW DOES IT... FEEL?
YEAH, I MEAN FALLING FOR A GUY.
I MEAN, SHINO, YOU'RE ALWAYS THE UKE.
THE ONE THAT TAKES IT.
U... UKE?!
When did he learn that word?
TAKES... IT?
SO, LIKE...
AND YOU'RE ALWAYS TAKING IT FROM TENRYU-SAN.
NAKAYA!
WHAT?
I DON'T KNOW WHY YOU'RE ASKING ALL THIS...
...BUT THIS NOT THE KIND OF TOPIC TO BE DISCUSSED AT THE DINNER TABLE!!
DAMMIT, SHINO, I'M BEING SERIOUS!

I'M NOT JUST SCREWING AROUND HERE!
... NAKAYA ...
I THOUGHT YOU OF ALL PEOPLE WOULD UNDERSTAND HOW I FEEL, SHINO!
HOW YOU FEEL ABOUT WHAT?
I...
I THINK I'M IN LOVE WITH A GUY.

WH...WHY NOW?!
HE LIKES A...
HUH?
...GUY ?!
ビクッ

WELL FINE, THEN!
EVERY LITTLE THING
I'M NOT ASKING FOR YOUR ADVICE ANYMORE!!
NAKA...!
BUT... YOU...
I THOUGHT YOU HAD A GIRLFRIEND.
YOUR GIRL-FRIEND ...
NAKAYA...

NAKAYA!
WAIT! WHERE ARE YOU GO--
WHAT'S IT TO YOU WHERE I GO?! LET GO OF ME!!
I KNEW IT.
YOU'RE JUST LIKE ALL THE OTHERS!
YOU KISSED TENRYU-SAN, DIDN'T YOU?!
WHY'D YOU DO THAT, SHINO?!

FILA SPORT
HE NEVER CAME BACK THAT NIGHT.
YOU'RE LATE, SHINO!
I JUST CALLED YOU!

'M SORRY...
WHAT'S WITH YOUR VOICE?
YOU HAVEN'T BEEN SLEEPING, HAVE YOU?!
AW, CRAP!
NOT GOOD!
'M SORRY.
AND IT DOESN'T HELP THAT YOU'RE A MAIN CHARACTER!
'M SORRY.
I'M GOING BACK TO THE OFFICE.
YOU JUST DO YOUR BEST IN THERE, SHINO!
... YESSIR.
OKAY.
TESTING. TESTING.
SORRY I'M LATE...
OH.
MORNING, THERE.

"IN THAT CASE, JUST HOW TO YOU INTEND TO CONVINCE ME?"
I CAN'T HELP FEELING DEPRESSED ABOUT ALL THIS.
"DO YOU REALLY WANT TO KNOW?"
......
KATORI-KUN...
HI...
"I THINK I DO."
"AH... NNG..."
"WH... WHAT'RE YOU...STOP IT! WHY'RE YOU PUTTING YOUR HANDS AROUND MY WAIST?!"
BUT WHERE COULD NAKAYA HAVE RUN OFF TO?
"IT'S... NOT THAT..."
"THEN I WON'T HOLD BACK."
"AAH... AH..."
"YOU DON'T LIKE IT?"

YOU KISSED TENRYU-SAN, DIDN'T YOU?!
WHY'D YOU DO THAT, SHINO?!
"TURN THIS WAY."
"CLOSE YOUR EYES."
SHINO.
SHINO!
WHAT'S WRONG?
YOU'RE UP NEXT.
R...
RIGHT...

......
DING DONG
NAKAYA?!
HEY.
TE... TENRYU-SAN.

YOU'VE BEEN ACTING STRANGE ALL DAY.
I DIDN'T MEAN TO WORRY YOU.
SHINO.
YOU KNOW, I'M HAPPY TO LISTEN TO YOUR PROBLEMS, SO IF THERE'S SOMETHING ON YOUR MIND, JUST TELL ME.
DID SOMETHING HAPPEN?
YEAH...
IT'S ABOUT YOUR SON, ISN'T IT?
ギクッ
WHAT? WHAT HAPPENED?
HE GET HIS GIRLFRIEND PREGNANT?
WE ALREADY RESOLVED THAT PROBLEM!
OKAY THEN, HE FELL FOR A GUY, DIDN'T HE?
HOW DID YOU...
...KNOW THAT...?
SO, HE HASN'T COME HOME SINCE LAST NIGHT?

YOU'RE NOT SURPRISED, TENRYU-SAN?
OH, I AM.
WELL YOU SURE DON'T LOOK IT.
I'M WONDERING IF THE REASON NAKAYA TURNED OUT LIKE THIS...
...IS BECAUSE OF MY JOB.
DON'T YOU THINK THAT'S KIND OF...
...AN OVERLY SIMPLISTIC CONCLUSION?
I...I SUPPOSE YOU'RE RIGHT.
SHINO.

...YES?
I'M IN LOVE WITH YOU.
...HICCUP.
NEXT TIME YOU CO-STAR WITH ME...
...I WANT YOU TO SYNCHRONIZE WITH ME.
WHEN I EMBRACE YOU... MAKE LOVE TO YOU... SHAME YOU...

P-PLEASE, STOP PLAYING WITH ME!
I'M NOT PLAYING WITH YOU.
WHAT'RE YOU GOING TO DO, SHINO?
UNLIKE YOUR SON, I WON'T RUN AWAY.
WHA...WHEN DID OUR CONVER-SATION TURN INTO THIS?!
YOU TEMPTED ME.
I DIDN'T DO ANYTHING ...!

WHAT ABOUT YOU?
TE... TENRYU ...
SHINO.
DING DONG
SORRY FOR COMING BY SO LATE AT NIGHT.
MY NAME IS FUSE.
I'M LOOKING FOR NAKAYA-KUN'S FATHER...

UM...DID SOMETHING HAPPEN TO NAKAYA...?
OH... ACTUALLY ...
REALLY?
THAT'S ME...
HE'S BEEN AT MY PLACE SINCE LAST NIGHT. I TRIED TO CONTACT YOU, BUT...
I SEE...I'M SO SORRY HE'S CAUSED YOU SO MUCH TROUBLE.
NOT AT ALL.
IT'S FINE. I LIVE ALONE.
NAKAYA!
I SAID, I'M NOT GOING HOME!!

I'M STAYING AT AKIHI'S HOUSE!
I'M NOT COMING BACK HERE.
Na... Nakaya...
LET'S... TALK THIS OUT.
I'VE GOT NOTHING MORE TO SAY TO YOU!
NAKAYA!
JUDGING BY THE CIRCUMSTANCES... I SUPPOSE I CAN LET HIM STAY AT MY PLACE FOR A WHILE...
BUT...
IT'S OKAY.
OH, BY THE WAY, I'M THE JUNIOR COACH OF THE GERONIMO CLUB, SO IF SOMETHING COMES UP, FEEL FREE TO CONTACT ME.
YOUR SON LIKES THE PRETTY ONES.
YEAH...
H-HEY! THAT'S NOT THE PROBLEM HERE!!

...WHAT DO YOU REALLY THINK I SHOULD DO?
IT'S JUST A PHASE.
IS THAT YOUR FAVORITE PHRASE, TENRYU-SAN?!
You said the same thing last time!
THINK ABOUT YOURSELF, SHINO.
NAKAYA IS NOT A KID ANYMORE.
YOU TWO MAY BE LIVING TOGETHER, BUT THERE WILL COME A DAY WHEN HE NO LONGER NEEDS YOU TO BE A PARENT.
BUT UP UNTIL NOW I HAVEN'T EVEN GOTTEN ONE THING RIGHT AS HIS FATHER!

BESIDES...
DON'T YOU THINK YOU MIGHT EVENTUALLY FIND SOMEONE WHO IS MORE IMPORTANT TO YOU THAN A SON?
B... BUT...
I'VE PRETTY MUCH FORGOTTEN ABOUT MY CHILD, AND I'M SURE IT'S THE SAME ON HER END.
I'LL SEE YOU LATER.
TENRYU... SAN?
YOUR DAD REALLY SURPRISED ME. I CAN'T BELIEVE HOW YOUNG HE LOOKS.
JUST HOW OLD IS HE?
THIRTY-THREE...

THIRTY-THREE?!
HUH? WAIT, BUT YOU'RE SEVENTEEN!
WHAT'S MY DAD MATTER TO YOU?
WELL...
HOW COME YOU'RE FIGHTING?
WHAT HAPPENED?
プシュ
...
I LIKE YOU.

WELL, I DON'T LET GUYS I DON'T LIKE STAY IN MY HOUSE, SO...
I TOLD YOU THAT ALREADY. BUT YOU SHOULD STILL GO HOME SOON...
A...
AKIHI.
WHAT, WE'RE ON A FIRST-NAME BASIS AFTER ONE NIGHT?

?
WHA...!
YOU...
NAKAYA!!

LET ME GO!
YOU IDIOT!!
IF YOU THINK YOU CAN JUST WRITE ME OFF...
...GO AHEAD AND TRY!
IT'LL BE GOOD TRAINING FOR ME! KEEP ME FROM GETTING BLOWN OVER SO EASILY!

WAI...!
NN...!
NA... NAKA...!
G-GET OFF OF ME!
NAKAYA!
MY KNEE...!

HAA
HAAH
HAA
HFF
HAA
Y...YOU...
YOU LIED TO ME...
HAAH
HAA
OH LIKE THAT'S WHAT'S WRONG WITH THIS PICTURE!!
I'VE BEEN TELLING YOU SINCE LAST NIGHT THAT I LIKE YOU.
BUT YOU'RE THE ONE WHO WON'T BOTHER TO LISTEN TO ME AND TELL ME HOW YOU FEEL!

WHAT HE... MEANS...
JUST YOU TRY AND PROVOKE ME...
...AND NEXT TIME I'LL GO ALL THE WAY WITH YOU!

GOOD NIGHT.
'NIGHT!
OH! AREN'T YOU DONE FOR THE NIGHT YET, HISAE-SAN?
OH...YEAH, I HAVE ABOUT TWO OR THREE MORE SOLO TAKES LEFT.
HISAE-SAN, IF KATORI KOUSUKE'S CAUSING YOU ANY PROBLEMS, JUST LET ME KNOW.
HUH?
I KNOW THAT HE'S ALL BUDDY-BUDDY WITH TENRYU-SAN, AND THAT HE SEES YOU AS A RIVAL, HISAE-SAN.

WHY WOULD HE FEEL THAT...?
BECAUSE YOU'RE DOING IT WITH TENRYU-SAN!
MI--
...
HEY.
YOU'RE NOT DENYING IT.
MI...
MIZU--
HERE YOU GO.
...SA... WA-KUN.
"Mizu"= water
ドキ
ドキ
I WANT TO GET TO KNOW YOU BETTER, HISAE-SAN.
SOMEONE YOUNGER WITH A SIMPLE AND CLEAR LIFE IS BETTER THAN ANY MIDDLE-AGED MAN AND ALL THAT BAGGAGE.
I THOUGH YOU PREFERRED YOUNGER PARTNERS, MIZUSAWA-KUN.

HISAE... SAN?
WHY DON'T YOU RUN ALONG HOME?
Pitiful...
WHAT IS THIS... JUST WHAT IS THIS?
EVER SINCE THAT HAPPENED, JUST HEARING TENRYU-SAN'S NAME MAKES MY CHEST HURT.
BUT HOW AM I SUPPOSED TO KEEP A LEVEL HEAD WHEN I'M WORKING WITH HIM SO MUCH?
IT'S ALL BECAUSE...
...HE JUST HAS TO BE SUCH A GREAT KISSER.

ARGH! HISAE SHINO, WHAT ARE YOU SAYING?!
Hisae-san?
OH!
GOOD EVENING.
HOW LONG HAVE YOU BEEN WAITING HERE...
...UH...
IT'S FUSE. SORRY FOR BARGING IN LIKE THIS.
OH, PLEASE COME RIGHT IN. YOU MUST BE COLD.

NOW THAT I'VE GOTTEN A GOOD LOOK AT HIM...
...I HAVE TO ADMIT, HE'S QUITE HANDSOME.
SORRY FOR TROUBLING YOU.
UH, HAS NAKAYA ...
...BEEN CAUSING ANY PROBLEMS ?
NO...
IT'S JUST...
YOU'RE A HOCKEY PLAYER TOO, RIGHT FUSE-SAN?
YES...
I USED TO PLAY ON THE CANADIAN TEAM SOME YEARS AGO...
CANADA ...?
YOU MEAN, YOU WENT ABROAD?
ACTUALLY! NAKAYA'S BEEN WATCHING THIS ONE VIDEO LATELY...
I COULD'VE SWORN IT WAS THE CANADIAN TEAM THAT WAS ON IT.

HUH?
SEE?
IT'S THIS ONE RIGHT HERE.
THE NORTH AMERICAN HOCKEY LEAGUE...
I DON'T KNOW HOW MANY TIMES HE'S WATCHED IT BY NOW.
I BELIEVE HE SAID THERE WAS A JAPANESE PLAYER ON THE HOT BOMBERS, THE CANADIAN TEAM FROM QUEBEC.
HMM ...

THAT WAS... ME.
IS THAT ...
...SO...
THEN... THAT MUST MEAN... THIS IS THE GUY NAKAYA LIKES...
HISAE-SAN.
I'M...
I'M GAY.
AND IT'S POSSIBLE THAT I MAY FEEL FOR NAKAYA-KUN WHAT HE FEELS FOR ME.

WOULD IT BE ALL RIGHT WITH YOU...
...IF I RETURNED THOSE FEELINGS?
WHAT?!
#6 END

Afterword

ヒラッ
...I returned those feelings?
Would it be all right with you...
What?!
WHAT DO YOU THINK, EVERYONE?
DOESN'T IT JUST KNOCK THE WIND OUT OF YOU?
OH, I JUST LOVE CLIFF-HANGERS!
Couldn't agree more.
I'M WITH YA'!
That's right!
UH-HUH! UH-HUH!
SORRY, SENSEI... WE ALL LIED (AGAIN)...
It sucks! It's over-done!
The ONE honest person...

But still...I really can't help but love cliff-hangers...heh heh...

Shout Out Loud!! 2nd Volume!!

Yahoo! Yay!! It's the 2nd issue of Shout Out Loud! that you've all been waiting for!!! Oh my, it looks like this time around even Nakaya has his problems to deal with... Oh my!! Here on in, the future is a blur! I'm just itching to see what happens!!!

But, Sensei...Kuniwaki hardly made an appearance in this volume. It's sad. Please give him more spotlight!

Actually, Mizusawa's also an uke.
I...THE TRUTH IS...
TENRYU-SAN IS AN UKE.
Hirohiko → Nozoko
It can't be!! Nakaya's totally an uke! Liiiiies! ALL LIIIIES!!
LULU-SAN. LULU-SAN.
Andy → Me
WHAT ?!
Shout Out Loud! Chapter six rough pages
NAKAYA'S A SEME?!
Manager Lulu, a papa who scorns youths who scream too easily, proofs the gay content.
BLU TRIVIA seme → The person that gives it uke → The person that takes it ok?
I know you're a seme!
I'M NOT.
P-PLEASE DON'T TOY WITH ME!
SHINO.
ACTUALLY, I'M AN UKE.
YOU'RE WRONG.
You fool!!
Tristan → Teacher
HE'S THE...
...SUPER-UKE!!
He was taken!
PLEASE CONTINUE TO NEXT VOLUME 2 AFTERWORD!

Mizusawa-kun...

Nozoko (sub-coordinator)
Was in the middle of work,
so no time for revisions...

I'm Mizusawa Terushi, the Uke Hunter.
E heh heh heh...
When it comes to ukes...
...I mow 'em down...?
Papa
When it comes to ukes...
I hunt 'em...?!
Papa
And if you're wondering what my worries are...
...I'll just tell you, "There are none."
I wonder if Sensei will forgive me...
D...don't insult our work!
It's all good...?!
When it comes to this profession, I'm like my name says: "only shining intentions."
...?
Don't give up, Terushi! After all, he's the one you love most of all! Live up to your name!

Late for a Date with the Devil
by Makimaki
ウイイ・・・ン
MIYUKI, why must you hate me like this?
Guess I'll just go home.
What's gotten into me?
NOO!!!
Listen, Maki...
You came to the arcade today to get pictures taken, right? What're you going to do if you spend all your coins on plushies, instead?
Drat this kid...
Manager Sunaya-san
I'm not going home until I get HiroyuXX!!
Even though I've already spent 1600yen on this stupid machine, I just can't get him!!
[NOTE: 1600yen is around $16. HA!]
In the end I didn't get her (not a single one).
But I managed somehow.
That's what you always do!
Ufu!
You wouldn't believe what I saw yesterday, Nakaya...
Hm?

Lately, I've been removed from "Shout Out Loud"...Yep...it's because my style doesn't fit...
Heh. You knew it...You knew it all along, Sensei...

SHOUT OUT LOUD! VOL. 2

Created by Satosumi Takaguchi

© 1997 Satosumi Takaguchi. All Rights Reserved. First published in Japan in 1997.

English text copyright ©2006 BLU

All rights reserved. No portion of this book may be reproduced or transmitted in any form or by any means without written permission from the copyright holders. This manga is a work of fiction. Any resemblance to actual events or locales or persons, living or dead, is entirely coincidental.

ISBN: 1-59816-317-5

First Printing: August 2006

10 9 8 7 6 5 4 3 2 1

Printed in Canada

NEXT TIME IN

SHOUT OUT LOUD!™

Nakaya, confused about his feelings for Fuse, takes a break from paternal advice by staying with his grandmother. The line between love and lust isn't an easy one to draw when you're seventeen, but even supposedly grown-up Shino is having a rough time of it. On his own after several months of having a permanent houseguest, Shino's apartment seems a little too big and empty for comfort, and somehow he ends up in a hotel with Tenryu... But nothing heats relationships up faster than a trip to the hot springs! The cast of Galactic Legend of the Three Kingdoms heads out for a relaxing weekend break at a local resort, and it's hard for the four leads to keep the drama of the series out of their own lives.

Follow the love lives of Izumi, Takamiya and others as they are brought together at a host club called "Blue Boy" that specializes in high-class male escorts. Love lines cross, chances are lost and found, and hearts are broken in this fan favorite boys' love classic.
LOVE MODE
Yuki Shimizu
1
BLU
In stores now! $9.99
BLU
FOR MATURE AUDIENCES ONLY
For information about where to buy BLU MANGA titles, visit www.BLUMANGA.com
©YUKI SHIMIZU

Here's a dog that will make you beg...

MAN'S BEST FRIEND
—INU MO ARUKEBA—
KAZUSA TAKASHIMA

When Ukyo rescues a stray dog and names it Kuro, he soon learns that he may have found a rare breed—his new dog can talk and magically transform into a hunky human! With his dog now taking the form of a hot man and licking him in various places, what is Ukyo to do?!

From the creator of BLU's Wild Rock.

FOR MATURE AUDIENCES ONLY
Price: $9.99
Available Now!

For information about where to buy BLU MANGA titles, visit www.BLUMANGA.com

© KAZUSA TAKASHIMA

MATURE

BLU

stop

blu manga are published in the original japanese format

go to the other side and begin reading